Snore, Dinosaur, Snore!

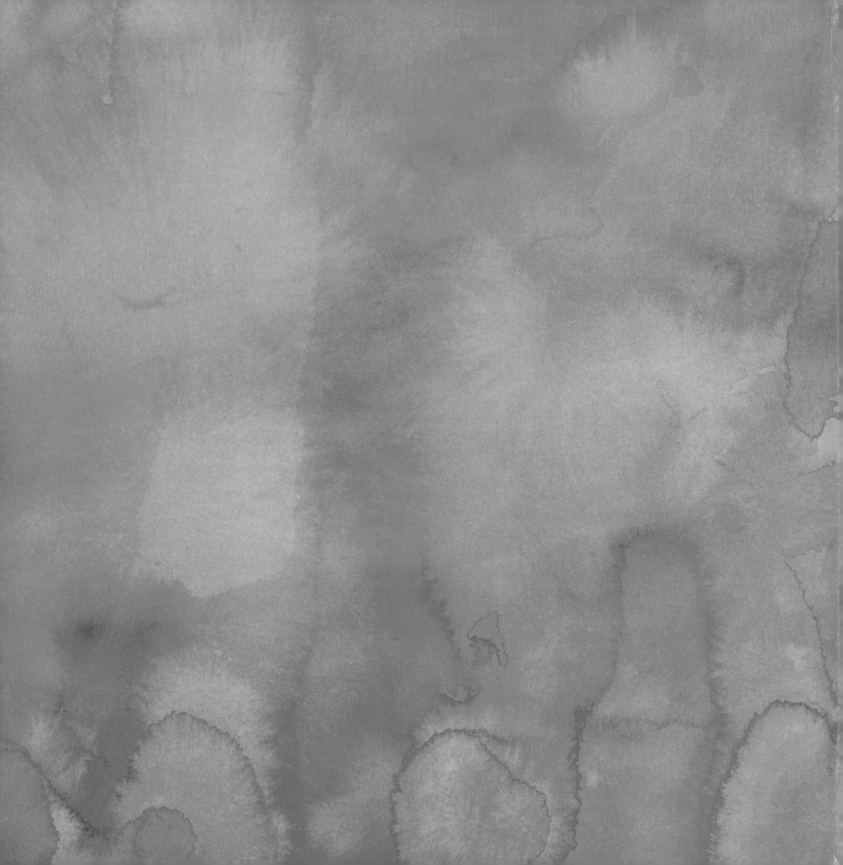

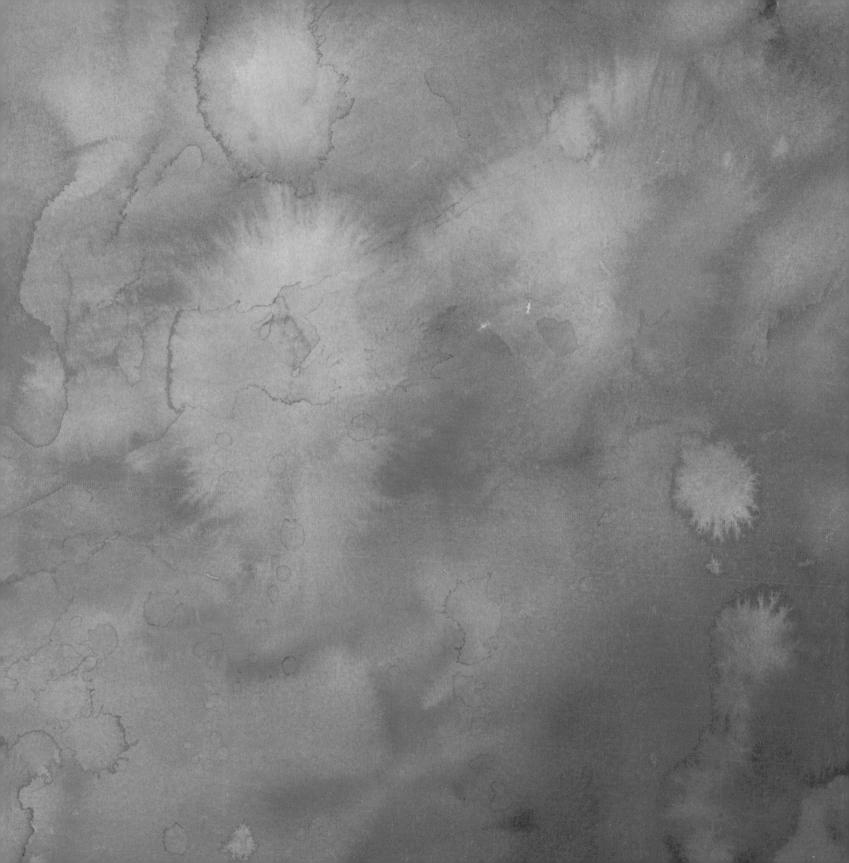

For Tiziana, as ever

John Bendall-Brunello

Snore, Dinosaur, Snore!

MARSHALL CAVENDISH CHILDREN

stretch

wake up!

elbow

run

roll

slide

snore

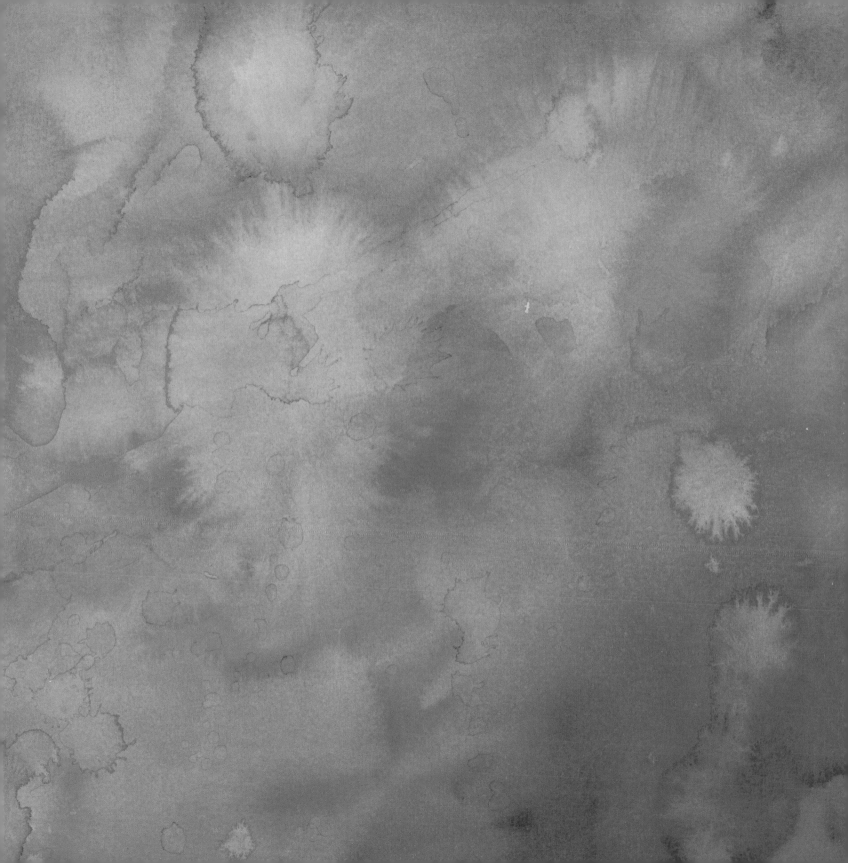

First published in Great Britain in 2009 by Andersen Press Ltd., 20 Vauxhall Bridge Road,
London SW1V 2SA.
Copyright © John Bendall-Brunello, 2009
First Marshall Cavendish Pinwheel Books edition, 2009
Marshall Cavendish Corporation, 99 White Plains Road, Tarrytown, NY 10591
www.marshallcavendish.us/kids

Pinwheel Books

Library of Congress Cataloging-in-Publication Data

Bendall-Brunello, John.
[Dinosnore!]
Snore, dinosaur, snore! / by John Bendall-Brunello. -- 1st Marshall Cavendish ed.
p. cm.
Originally published: Dinosnore!. Great Britain : Andersen Press Ltd.
Summary: Three little dinosaurs try several different ways to wake their sleeping mother.
ISBN 978-0-7614-5626-1
[1. Snoring--Fiction. 2. Mother and child--Fiction. 3. Dinosaurs--Fiction. I. Title.
PZ7.B43135Sn 2009 [E]--dc22
2008053636

10   9   8   7   6   5   4   3   2   1
Original book design by Photolithe AG, Zürich

Printed in Malaysia

mc Marshall Cavendish
Children